The Gift
of
Urr

The Gift
of
Urr

by

Larry Nalder

ISBN: 1-55517- 502-3
v.1

Published by Bonneville Books

Distributed by:
925 North Main, Springville, UT 84663 • 801/489-4084

Typeset by Virginia Reeder
Cover design by Adam Ford
Cover design © 2000 by Lyle Mortimer

Printed in the United States of America

PROLOGUE

The Smarzon explorers aboard the spaceship, "THE HOPE," have traveled outside their galaxy for three thousand years on a mission to explore the universe. Everything in their path, even minute pieces of matter, have not missed their intense scrutiny. They have searched for one thing, an extremely rare substance, called "URLA." The seventy-five remaining crew members are weary from their many years of exploration. Most expect to live and continue this vital mission for at least a thousand more years and even with this much time, their life's mission could end in failure. Lack of their success will mean extinction of the Smarzons forever.

They have explored this new planet for two full revolutions around its sun and are almost finished. Because of the similarities this planet has with their planet, called "SMAR," they have taken more time in their exploration. They hope that URLA might be found and they can return home. Sadly, this planet also fails to contain the URLA substance. However, it does contain a great abundance of water, plants, numerous living creatures, and a life form with the ability to reason. During their years of exploration, this is a first. These life forms are primitive but in many ways resemble themselves. THE HOPE'S crew feels a kinship with them.

One of the crew members known as "URR" senses his time to die is near. Like many of the previous crew that have died, he requests his remaining time be spent on the surface of the planet they are now exploring. He also requests that this planet be named "URR'TH," the name to be derived by adding "TH" to his name to include the name of their spacecraft "THE HOPE."

A Smarzon's ring is their most cherished possession. It provides them with special powers and knowledge that have enabled them to be the most supreme beings of the universe. Upon death, it is customary that a Smarzon's ring be removed and retained aboard the spacecraft for the return back to SMAR. URR will break this custom. He will look for a worthy URR'TH inhabitant and leave him his ring. He prepares to leave the spaceship and live his remaining time on the planet he has named "URR'TH."

URR'S DEPARTURE

It was dusk when the spacecraft hovered fifty feet above the planet's surface. The crew commander chose a tree and rock-protected mountain meadow for Urr to depart. Urr, and most of the spaceship's occupants would soon gather for a moment outside the protection of their spacecraft. Once on the Earth's surface, they would wish him a sad and final farewell. It was always difficult to lose a crew member, especially URR who will be one most missed, a sad loss for all those who must continue this mission.

Because the crew were old, travel weary, and homesick, they decided URR could retain his ring, making him the first Smarzon ever to permanently exit the spacecraft with a ring. Another consideration was the planet's inhabitants who possessed the ability to reason. They found satisfaction in knowing the power and knowledge contained in "The Ring," would not be lost forever.

THE GIFT OF
URR

Chapter 1

NACHEZWA (Son of a Fallen Leader)

Nachezwa found solace being away from his camp. He was filled with grief from the recent loss of his father, Eagle Feather. He sought comfort in the memory of his father, friend, and teacher. He remembered the patience his father showed while teaching him the necessary hunting skills. The knowledge of these skills was important because he soon would have to prove himself. The warriors must have proof before they would accept him as one of them. He also knew that if he didn't return to camp soon, his mother's concern would turn to worry. His camp was a short distance from his favorite secluded mountain meadow. If he started back now he could return before dark and Bird Wing's worries would all disappear. As he reached the uppermost ledge, he turned to look at the beauty of the meadow when a large shadow passed over his head. Instinctively, he dove to the ground seeking cover from the large strange object that suddenly appeared out of the heavens. It looked as if it were going to land itself upon the grass that covered the meadow floor.

Nachezwa lay incredibly still, unable to believe what he was seeing. He remained well hidden. To the best of his young memory, never before had something such as this ever been discussed. Not by his father or any of the tribe's people. From his lofty position he could see the big bird-like object. It appeared bigger than all the tribe's teepees combined. Nachezwa estimated it to be as long as the line of horses they used in moving their entire camp. It was also more than five horses high. Slowly the large object began to settle closer to the ground. It looked to Nachezwa as if it never did rest upon or touch the surface, but remained hovering a small distance above the ground. It made very little sound; only a muffled whirring could be heard. This sound was similar to the noise emitted by clouds of swampland mosquitoes. Relating this humming sound to that of the mosquitoes and knowing the pain and misery they could inflict caused him fear and concern. Yet, he did not run away; he wanted to see what the big object was preparing to do.

It was dusk and long dark shadows were beginning their ascent across the meadow. He knew he should be back to camp before dark or his mother, Bird Wing, would become alarmed. She worried about him because he had seen only fourteen summers of life. The strange object had many bright sun-like campfires. These small suns brightened the entire meadow. Nachezwa could see clearly as if this were occurring during mid day. He watched as the bottom side of the big object slowly opened. A blue-green light burst out and downward with such brightness it caused Nachezwa to shade and protect his eyes. Several small creatures, unlike anything he had ever seen, came out the opening and down through the eerie light. Gently they floated, like feathers, toward the surface below. All these creatures appeared to be very similar. In fact, Nachezwa could see few differences. Unlike the people of Nachezwa's tribe, he could see they were small, much smaller than himself. He observed they were more in total numbers than members of his tribe.

Their bodies were a blend of blues, greys, and

greens. Instead of arms, legs, fingers and feet, they had small, orange-colored nodules. Two nodules protruded from each socket where an arm and leg would normally exist. These nodules didn't appear sturdy enough to support even their small size. Their head was a pale orange, with black lines evenly spaced. The head had four protrusions with distinct colors. At the end of the head protrusions extended a single small bright orange finger-like nodule. Those on top of the head were larger than those on the side. The front center of their head was tear-drop shaped and charcoal in color. The nose, lips and eyes were all a dark shiny black. The eyes were large, also tear-drop shaped, and slightly bulged out from their face. All wore a grey ring mass around their narrow elongated neck.

Nachezwa, as he continued to shield his eyes, noticed movement outside the area lit by the object's many campfires. Someone or something appeared to be stalking one of the creatures. It crept low against the ground, slowly coming within the area illuminated by the strange objects—many small suns. Nachezwa could then see the stalker to be the big mountain cat, the one with the crippled rear leg. Nachezwa, many times during play, and while hunting, had seen this big cat having difficulty capturing something to eat. Most game, in these mountains, were now quicker than this mountain lion. However, if he or any of the children of the tribe, remained unaware of it, they would be easy prey, even with its bad rear leg. Nachezwa knew this winter would prove difficult for the big cat. Its ability to catch and kill enough game to survive the winter would be severely tested. Extreme hunger must have driven it to prey upon these strange creatures. Even their large numbers and the bright lights of the big object's many camp fires did not discourage him. Emitting a loud scream it ran forward. It remained low to the ground until it sprang high in the air with the intention of landing on top of its prey. It had selected the nearest creature. Somehow, much to Nachezwa's amazement, the cat was held suspended in mid flight. His screams drowned out the whirring noise made by the big strange object. The loud screams were somehow silenced. It appeared as if the creature somehow commanded the big cat to be silent. Several creatures floated around the large animal and some touched it with their strange looking feelers. Nachezwa watched the animal being poked as it was slowly rolled upside down while being held in mid air. Once they completed their examination, the creatures left the cat suspended. The creatures ignored the cat and formed a line only to pass one by one in front of one of their comrades. It was the one which the lion had selected but failed to make good on his attack. Their passing in front of the single creature appeared to be one of great sorrow and sadness, reminding him of how his tribe mourned over the death of his father. Unlike his tribe, no noise came from these creatures as they proceeded past the lone figure. As each completed this process, it then floated upward into the underbelly of the big object. Only the single creature remained, with its head bent low. The humming sound increased as the bottom of the big flying object proceeded to close. As it closed, the green light diminished until it also gave way to the dark. Nachezwa heard them increase the strength of the whirring sound. Colored lights shot out in all directions and the big object seemed to shudder. It slowly moved straight up, casting its eerie light on Nachezwa, as it quickly gathered momentum, until it disappeared into the heavens.

Barely able to see in the dim light of darkness,

Nachezwa arose from his hiding spot. He strained to see the creature and the lion, but the darkness had covered the meadow. However, his skyline silhouette did not go unobserved by the lion and the strange creature. Unaware of his mistake, he proceeded the short distance back to camp at a rapid pace, in spite of the darkness.

During his journey back to the camp, his thoughts were those of both excitement and concern. Excited over what he had seen, he was concerned that if he told the elders they would laugh at him and wouldn't believe him. They might make him wait another summer before considering him as a warrior. This he felt would crush his dream. Once a warrior, he could hunt with older warriors, sit in discussion and become a productive member of the tribe. As a warrior he would be required to provide the tribe with meat, furs, weapons, and horses. Yes, he felt it would be best for now that he keep what he had seen within himself.

As he came within view of the campfire, Bird Wing, and his uncle, Wolf Paw, showed signs of relief. Their expressions of relief soon gave way to those of displeasure that he had stayed away into the night. This was a known taboo, a rule long understood by him and all the tribe's young. Empty handed of small game, he could not offer any excuse. He knew Bird Wing had cause to worry, especially with the recent death of her husband, Eagle Feather. He could see that Wolf Paw was upset. At Bird Wing's request, Wolf Paw was about to mount his pony and search for Nachezwa. Wolf Paw directed a grunt and gesture of disapproval towards Nachezwa as he retired to his teepee. To avoid being scolded, Nachezwa hurriedly ate some dried meat, berries, and pemmican as he entered his teepee. Pretending to sleep, he knew, would delay Bird Wing's scolding until morning.

Early the next morning he was up before the sun. Quietly, he pulled on his moccasins and crept out of their encampment, trying not to arouse even the lightest of sleepers. Two camp dogs raised their heads with an unconcerned acknowledgment of his departure. The camp dogs were accustomed to the frequent comings and goings of the tribe's members. Neither dog offered up a bark or so much as a low growl. However, if a stranger approached the encampment, they would make a ruckus, barking and growling, until a tribe member would command them to be quiet. This was the sole purpose of the six or seven dogs kept in the camp; they would provide early warning of any approaching strangers and possible danger.

Once headed on an animal trail back to the meadow, Nachezwa began to wonder. Had he really seen the big flying object with it's many small creatures, it's flashing fires, and whirring sound? Maybe he had dreamed the entire event. He must prove to himself it wasn't a dream! This was what he must do, before attempting to explain the mysterious occurrence to others! He decided to return to the exact spot he had witnessed the previous day's happenings.

As he approached the meadow, he slowed his pace, taking precautions not to make a sound. He lay in the same spot as the day before. He could see where his body had left an imprint in the sparse grasses and dirt. He hadn't been dreaming! As time passed, he watched a covey of mountain grouse enter the meadow's furthest corner. He knew these birds were always alert; if they remained undisturbed, it was likely nothing of danger would catch him unaware. Like the camp dogs, they squawked a loud warning signal of danger. He determined it was safe to approach the area where the flying object had hovered above the ground. Nachezwa was taught, always be quiet and cautious when away from camp. He examined the area for any tracks that might have been left by the small creatures and the big flying object. None could be found! He discovered the spot where the mountain lion had begun his charge toward the strange creature. Upon his approach to this area; the mountain grouse sounded an alarm. A loud squabble, mixed with sharp clucking sounds, could be heard as they flew a short distance into the nearby thicket.

Once Nachezwa satisfied his curiosity, he sat upon a large rock to ponder the situation. This rock would allow him good observation in case of approaching danger. His mind raced with mixed thoughts of what to do. Sitting motionless and quiet, he could see the grouse cautiously working their way back into the meadow. They soon occupied the area from which they had previously retreated. As he watched the birds, he contemplated his return with a bird for supper. This might amend his situation with Bird Wing from the previous night.

He took careful aim with his arrow, pointed to strike the nearest bird. Before letting the arrow fly, from the corner of his eye, he detected movement. The mountain cat appeared in his side vision within a few feet of him. How could that be? The birds never gave warning! The small strange creature also came into view.

Chapter 2

NACHEZWA ENCOUNTERS URR

Overcome with fear, he attempted to leap off the rock. Unable to move, he was held in place; he couldn't even blink his eyes. His fear and panic was quickly replaced with a calm such as he had never before experienced. Both the lion and the creature came within touching distance. He couldn't move, but for some reason he didn't want to and he knew his mind and body were under the control of the creature. The mountain lion lay at the base of the boulder below his feet. It appeared more docile than the tribe's smallest and meekest camp dog. Without a spoken word the creature communicated through Nachezwa's mind. It assured him that no harm would come to him and he would soon be released. The creature explained that he was in the process of assimilating for himself all that was in Nachezwa's mind. He, Urr, then spoke using Nachezwa's native language. The sound of Nachezwa's own voice came forth from Urr, and assured him the cat would do no harm now or ever. How could he be sure? How did this creature speak in his native tongue? It was using the same voice as if he himself, Nachezwa, had uttered it! Urr, able to read Nachezwa's thoughts explained, "My tribe and I have been traveling for many seasons exploring planets and stars in the many heavens. We were in search of a material called "URLA." The material, URLA , is needed before my people can have offspring. Our place of origin no longer contains this rare substance. My traveling party was told by our chief to explore the many stars in search of this substance. Once found, we must return to our camp called SMAR, my place of birth. If my people do not soon find URLA, our people will no longer exist. It is near the end for my people back on SMAR." Nachezwa, the young Indian, was somehow made to understand this creature's quest for their life-giving substance URLA.

It was agreed, Nachezwa would return each evening to his tribe without revealing his encounters with Urr. During each of Urr's remaining days, he would teach Nachezwa of the power and knowledge contained with his ring. Because it was the fall season, days were short and darkness came early. Nachezwa would again be returning empty handed. His mother or uncle would surely scold him and require he remain at camp. If he didn't return soon he would be unable to meet with Urr in the future. Anytime now they would be preparing to move to lower ground before a winter storm settled in the area. As if by magic, one of the mountain grouse flew over their heads and collapsed. It fell dead, as if it had been shot with an arrow. The mountain lion hardly took notice. Nachezwa returned to his camp before dusk with the grouse hanging from his side. His mother was glad to see both him and the fowl. Being late the previous day was forgiven.

The camp was quieter than usual. Nachezwa didn't have to ask why. He knew the warriors were preparing for a last hunt on the mountain. They would hunt longer to obtain a large cache of meat and furs. The cold nights and cool days would preserve the meat for long periods of time. Sometimes the frozen meat would last until spring. All furs were stretched and preserved. The women did most of the work with the furs once they were removed from the animals. When the furs and hides were in proper condition, they made articles of clothing, a task at which the women far excelled the men.

All tribe members, except Dog Fang, knew how to make acceptable moccasins, leggings, hats, and other clothing used as protection from the cold winter storms. Bird Wing was exceptionally good at making moccasins. The making of moccasins required the most patience and skill in selecting the best of the leather hides. Each tribe member achieved great skills and developed expertise in various functions. Wolf Paw was the best hunter, Badger Face made the finest of bow and arrow. Walking Elk's ponies were well trained and were the most prized. Eagle Feather was excellent at getting the tribe to think and act as a unit. He organized the hunts, assigned the furs and game, decided when to move camp, and where to camp. They were so few in number they were hardly even large enough to be called a tribe. Counting men, women, and children, they fell two short of fifty. Eagle Feather had been viewed as leader by the people of their small tribe. With his untimely death, the tribe's warriors must decide who should assume his place. Wolf Paw, the one most likely, temporarily assumed responsibility. Wolf Paw accepted this position only to keep Dog Fang from making himself acting chief. The tribes people knew that they and four other tribes would be gathering at the winter camp. These five tribes would have council and the warriors would select a single chief over all the gathered tribes. Eagle Feather had been viewed as the most likely to become chief of all the tribes, had he not been killed. Even Dog Fang knew and would have accepted the choice of Eagle Feather as chief. With Eagle Feather gone he, Dog Fang, thought he should become chief of the five tribes. Dog Fang was always the cause of trouble. When he saw problems, he instinctively made them worse. Lacking in skills of value resulted in his goods being of no value for trade. His needs for meat, moccasins, arrows, horses, or any winter supplies were usually acquired in a devious manner. Dog Fang also had a streak of meanness, which he didn't keep well hidden. When he was unable to cause trouble within the tribe, he would often kick or hit the camp dogs with sticks and rocks. The camp dogs soon learned to avoid Dog Fang. They would always stay out of his way. Nachezwa didn't like Dog Fang. It made him angry that Dog Fang would continually try to persuade Bird Wing into trading his no-value items for a pair of her moccasins. Since Eagle Feather's death, Dog Fang spent more and more unwelcome time around Bird Wing and Nachezwa's teepee. Nachezwa thought to himself that when he became a warrior, he would deal with Dog Fang.

"When Nachezwa becomes a warrior." This thought was always on his mind. He would follow in his father's footsteps. Someday he would become chief and supreme leader. It was customary, after a season of hunts with the other warriors, to re-name the new warriors. They selected a name that he would be called for his remaining days. Nachezwa, like his father, was in awe of the eagle. It could fly long distances, possessed great speed, and had the ability to see even the smallest mouse while soaring hundreds of feet in the air. Speed, skill, and cunning, gave it the power to kill game much larger than itself. He knew the eagle had but few creatures to fear. Nachezwa wished, when he became a warrior, his new name would be associated with the mighty white-headed eagle.

Nachezwa had learned from his father to enjoy the mountains and the various seasons, even the harshness of winter. They had many warm furs that provided warmth. These furs, combined with heat from the small teepee fire, made winter sleep enjoyable. He knew it was during this time when he would most miss his father. In the cold winter months when they were confined to the teepee, his father taught him about animals, tribe members, and life's many trials. They were great companions. The bond between them appeared much stronger than most warriors and their sons.

It was already beginning to get cold, especially at night. Thinking of the absence of his father caused Nachezwa anxiety, especially concerning winter supplies and the moving to winter camp. He also worried about the survival of Urr, the small, strange creature. Urr didn't look strong and had no furs to keep him warm. His thoughts continued: "How will Urr survive in the near freezing temperatures without furs, shelter, and a fire?" He thought about the mountain lion. The mountain lion's rear leg appeared healed. Impossible! Again the thought came over him; was he really seeing these things or was it his imagination? He was going to ask Urr why the lion's leg was no longer broken. These concerns, combined with the days events, caused him to be overcome with exhaustion and he fell into a deep and restful sleep.

Bird Wing had taken notice of Nachezwa's early departures and late returns. Often, he was back by dusk or just at dark. She noticed it to be more so these last few days. He hardly took time to eat or show interest in the goings on in the camp. He never even inquired if Dog Fang, was stirring up trouble. Nachezwa's behavior didn't really worry or alarm Bird Wing, once she saw his safe return by night fall. Nachezwa was always a curious one. He seemed to enjoy being off by himself, especially when Eagle Feather was off hunting. None of the other young males were as old as Nachezwa. His closest companions were two summers younger. When they were nearly old enough to become warriors, hunting and exploring their surroundings were steps necessary to become one. Even his younger companions knew this was normal. Bird Wing tried not to show her concern, but with the loss of her husband, Nachezwa was the only important thing in her life she had left. She worried that he too could get killed or crippled. She worried about him falling prey to a bear, or even that big mountain lion with the broken rear leg, the one she often saw near camp. She noticed the mountain lion would often appear when the warriors were off hunting. It could be seen overlooking their camp, but always remaining at enough distance so it wouldn't alarm the camp dogs. She knew a wound would often make animals, even humans, mean and vicious, and cause them to hunt and act differently than healthy animals. That was the reason for their law; a hunter that wounded an animal had responsibility to continue the hunt and destroy that animal. That's why the bear managed to kill her husband Eagle Feather, although Wolf Paw had never revealed this to her or the other tribe members. It was Dog Fang's fault that Eagle Feather was killed by the bear. If Eagle Feather had killed the bear and survived, he and Wolf Paw had agreed to punish Dog Fang for being a coward. Eagle Feather's true cause of death was a secret known only by Wolf Paw and Dog Fang.

Nachezwa was too excited to eat anything; he wanted to get to the meadow to again be with Urr and the lion. As he approached the large rock outcropping that overlooked the meadow, he lifted off the ground. He floated, much to his amazement, to where Urr and the lion were waiting. He asked, when safely settled on the ground, "How did I come to float in the air like a feather? It was just as I saw your people do!" Urr spoke, in the same voice as Nachezwa's. "You will learn this and more in the next few days. I will be with you for just a short time. I want you to learn much, before I go." Nachezwa didn't have to ask why! Their minds were already linked as if they were one.

The question of how the lion became well was answered, as were others. Urr told Nachezwa, "The ability to heal is one of the many powers contained in the ring. All things you will see, feel and learn are contained within this ring you see around my neck." Without speaking, Urr was able to transfer information to Nachezwa. He became aware of the many powers provided by the ring, many of which he wouldn't, or couldn't use, during his brief life span. Further, he somehow knew the ring would not function for deeds with greedy and evil intent. Nachezwa asked, "How will the ring know if its powers are being requested for evil and greedy purposes?" Urr said, "The ring becomes part of the bearer's thought process; one cannot keep secrets from one's self. Even an evil person knows his true intentions. It will know whether one's intentions are to perform deeds of good or evil. This power was built into the ring many millions of years ago by our great forefathers. They witnessed what evil some would do when given such powers. Our leaders destroyed those rings. This ring will only serve its bearer for good purposes. Using this ring, your tribe's people will greatly improve. Your abilities to learn will increase. You will no longer have to contend with the many problems associated with greed and evil, as you now do with your disliked warrior Dog Fang." Nachezwa said, "How do you know about Dog fang?" Urr replied, "I know all that's in your mind! That is how I know about Dog Fang. The death of your father, your tribe's leader, killed by an animal you call a bear. I know all about your tribe because I know all that is within your mind."

Urr continued, "When you wear the ring, you will have access to much of the knowledge and powers we possess. Once I remove the ring from around my neck I will no longer live. My life of four thousand and twenty of your summers will end. We could have given your people all our knowledge, but this would require two rings which we did consider. We had many rings remaining from those who died during our long journey. We decided not to leave two rings because future people, living on this planet, will have to earn and gain knowledge as did our people."

Chapter 3

ABOUT THE RING OF URR

At birth, this ring was placed around Urr's neck. The ring acquires and retains the characteristics of those who wear it. The strongest influence is derived from the first one to wear the ring. Urr, having been first to wear this ring, has forever imprinted himself within the ring's memory. This is the only Smarzon ring ever allowed to exist outside their society. It will always be known by its bearer as : "THE RING OF URR."

Urr's memory will forever remain within the ring and provide its bearer Urr's influence and guidance. Some of the characteristics and powers of the ring are:

Cure the sick.

Provide its bearer warm/cool shelter.

Allow you, and those chosen by you, the ability of flight.

Allow you to read one's mind, with or without their knowledge.

Let you suspend or immobilize any moving object.

Let you make someone or something perform acts

against their will, proven the bearer's intentions are good.

Let you empower within your eyes a powerful beam of light which can be used in many ways, even to destroy evil.

Let you move objects with brain thoughts.

Provide you with the memory of Urr for logical answers to all questions.

Will never cease to function, as long as the bearer's intentions are for good.

Will not perform deeds of greed and evil.

Is indestructible.

Adapt itself to fit the one who wears it.

Cause pain to befall the bearer if deeds are intended for ill intent.

Know its bearer's intentions.

Allow the bearer to become invisible.

Nachezwa's head swirled with all this knowledge. Although he was anxious to wear the ring, he did not wish for Urr's death. Urr, knowing Nachezwa's thoughts, told him that he would soon become the bearer of the ring. Urr then reviewed events that Nachezwa had already observed. Both the cat and Nachezwa had been held suspended; the cat in mid air; Nachezwa above the rock;

the cat was healed and its hunger was satisfied. The mountain grouse, that fell dead at Nachezwa's feet, sacrificed itself to nourish both Bird Wing and Nachezwa. Urr then directed his vision to a large boulder some fifty yards away. A narrow beam of yellow blue light shot from Urr's eyes and struck the boulder. It shattered into several small pieces. Urr explained to Nachezwa that the ring provided him with a protective barrier. If the mountain lion had been allowed to complete his charge, it would have struck Urr's invisible protective barrier, further injuring the broken leg. "To prevent this from happening, the lion was held in mid air and remained so until my farewell ceremony was completed." Urr explained that he had been comfortable, day and night, even when it became cold. Urr had made himself invisible, and while invisible, he spoke from behind Nachezwa. He explained that he and his people were aware of Nachezwa lying motionless on that upper ledge viewing the farewell ceremony. He continued to explain, "You, Nachezwa, were previously chosen to be the wearer of my ring. While we explored this planet, we read the minds of many people in the nearby tribes. You, and the people of your tribe, also had your minds read without knowing. We selected you, Nachezwa, to become the one to wear my ring. Because of you, I left my people that night.

Urr made himself visible and told Nachezwa he only had two more days of life remaining. For this remaining period, he would explore the beautiful surroundings of these mountains. Urr told Nachezwa to meet him again, in this meadow, in two days. "It will be when I turn the ring over to you." Urr released his power over the mountain lion, allowing it to go its own way. Once the cat had reached a short distance, it turned and paused to look back at Urr and Nachezwa. The look was as if to give thanks that I am well again!" It then scampered over the rocks and into the thicket, showing no signs of ever having a broken rear leg.

"See you in two days," Nachezwa said to Urr as he slowly floated upward and over the tall pines and disappeared from view. Nachezwa sat upon that same large rock and thought about all that had happened since he had met Urr. Thoughts of what he could do with the ring's powers filled his head.

After a period of time, he made his way slowly back to his camp. He was overcome with emotion he'd never before experienced. While his mind raced with thoughts of wearing the ring, he also felt waves of sadness. This small creature, with much wisdom, would in two days no longer live. This overwhelmed him with uncontrolled emotions of sorrow. If this had happened earlier this summer, the ring's power could have saved his father's life.

After having only known Urr for such a brief time, he felt he had always known him and the plight of his people. He thought, once a warrior, one must be brave. Sorrow and fear were emotions allowed only for women and children. No one must ever see these in him if he is to become a true warrior. Knowing he was alone, and not yet a warrior, he allowed those feelings of sorrow to overwhelm him. Sitting beneath a lofty pine, he cried softly. Only the cool autumn breeze, and two squirrels, busily gathering nuts, witnessed the relieving sobs of this grief-stricken young Indian.

Chapter 4

A CHANGED NACHEZWA

Time passed; it would soon be dark. Nachezwa entered camp still feeling sad and unworthy to be a warrior. He was ashamed of having cried as he did when he was young. He planned to quietly slip undetected into his teepee.

Glancing about, the camp appeared deserted. A deserted camp aroused his curiosity. Instead of entering his teepee as planned, he cautiously moved about the other teepees. What he saw as he wandered about camp caused a change; a quiet calm replaced his feelings of weakness. He observed a tranquil scene of animal hides, stretched in preparation for use this winter, the tribe's women and their young sitting at the far end of camp, their backs toward Nachezwa. They were all listening to Bird Wing. He crept near enough to listen and still remain unobserved. Bird Wing was explaining what each family must do to prepare for the move to the lower valley. They would prepare for a trip lasting several day's, carrying all their possessions. He was impressed with Bird Wing's instructions. She explained how they, as a tribe, were to assemble at the winter gathering of the many tribes. Nachezwa remained hidden and continued to listen to his mother, watching her every gesture. He found deep interest in what his mother was saying, now more than ever. Nachezwa thought how his deceased father had instructed the tribe on these matters. His mother's leadership appeared to be as good or even wiser. How did Bird Wing become so knowledgeable, able to command everyone's attention, even that of the smallest child. Nachezwa's eye saw what his father's eyes had seen for the many seasons of their union. He discovered that his father did not alone accomplish the many great feats, much knowledge and strength came from the hidden greatness of his mother. From that moment on, Bird Wing would unknowingly command great respect from her son, never again to be taken lightly.

For the next two days, Nachezwa found himself doing things he had seldom done before. Without prodding, he assisted his mother and several of the tribe women with their daily chores. He entertained the small children with stories of how to become the best of warriors. Nachezwa soon became the talk of the tribe's women, much to the surprise of Bird Wing. While Nachezwa gathered firewood the women talked; no youngster had ever been so helpful, this was unheard of. All were pleased, yet swore secrecy, to never openly mention Nachezwa's acts of kindness. Warriors such as Dog Fang would surely find fault and cause trouble. The camp dogs even seemed to trust Nachezwa; he often provided them with food and allowed some of his time to join in their play. The smallest dog, the one he called POT DOG, became very attached to him and Bird Wing. "Pot Dog" earned his name because his body looked much like the tribe's many clay pots. Even the camp dogs showed a newly gained appreciation for the new Nachezwa.

It was mid morning and near time to rendezvous at the meadow with Urr. He wandered out of camp in the opposite direction, pretending to search for firewood. With the added attention to the tribe's children, he had acquired a devoted following. He managed to at last discourage Pot Dog, along with the last of his young followers. He made a circular journey around the camp's outer perimeter to assure himself he had no followers. He moved at a brisk pace toward the meeting place with Urr. He was excited to meet with Urr. Nachezwa knew Urr was old and he reluctantly accepted Urr's predicted death. The ring would soon be his.

Nachezwa never left the camp without his bow and arrows and the crude, but sharp, flint knife given to him by Badger Face. The weapons were always with him to help him hunt and for protection from bears, cougars, wolves and badgers. Cautiously, he approached the rocky ledge that overlooked the meadow; he became alert; sensing danger. He crept forward with added caution, bow and arrow ready, slowly proceeding toward the end of the ledge. Looking down at the rock where he was told to meet Urr, stood the largest grizzly bear he had ever seen. This bear was much larger than the one that had killed his father. Wolf Paw had skinned and prepared that one's hide to keep them warm on cold winter nights. The bear vigorously pawed the ground behind the rock. The bear was unaware of Nachezwa and continued with his angry pawing, while emitting loud snorts and growls. Most of its body and its furious activity remained hidden from Nachezwa's view by the large rock. Nachezwa, even though fascinated by the size and strength of this magnificent animal, still wished Urr would soon appear and send the large animal on its way. A thought came to his mind; if he could kill this bear, he would no longer have to wait to become a warrior. No story was ever told where a single warrior killed a bear by himself, and lived to tell about it. Until Urr appeared, Nachezwa remained content in watching the mighty bear's activity. He was so transfixed in watching the bear, he failed to see the mountain lion, the one Urr had healed. The lion was also curious about the bear's activity and he remained unaware of Nachezwa. They were separated by rocks and underbrush, hidden from each others view. Both were curious as to what was hidden behind that rock to so infuriate the bear. His mind's question and the lion's curiosity was answered when the bear's powerful thrust threw high into the air the hidden thing that seemed to anger it. Seeing the lifeless body of Urr being tossed into the air by this gigantic animal infuriated Nachezwa. Without thinking, he let out with a loud bellow, full of rage.

The grizzly, hearing Nachezwa's loud retort, stopped pawing and stood up on his hind feet. Sniffing and looking in the direction of Nachezwa, it squinted with its poor-sighted eyes, still snorting with rage. Something dared to disturb his mauling of this small, lifeless body. The lion recognized the object to be Urr; it also issued forth with a loud angry scream. It being the fall season, nothing should challenge a full-grown bear, especially this bear. Anything and everything seemed to make it angry. In the fall season bears have a ferocious appetite, devouring everything they come upon. With winter near, they require much stored fat to maintain them during their long period of hibernation. Before hibernation, the ferocious appetite dictated his cantankerous behavior. Once Nachezwa and the lion had challenged the bear, they then realized just how large and powerful this animal was. Nachezwa also knew he didn't have the power of the ring. The ring, he could see, still remained around Urr's neck. The bear, fully aware of both the lion and Nachezwa, was deciding how to meet this new challenge. It was at this same time that Nachezwa and the lion became aware of each other. Another loud bellow of rage rang forth.

Nachezwa took aim and let fly with an arrow, striking the giant in the left shoulder. The bear swung furiously at it with its paw, breaking the arrow with half of the shaft left remaining in its shoulder. Nachezwa quickly placed another arrow in his twisted deer-hide bow string. With little hesitation, the bear came at full gallop up the steep hillside. Loud grunting and bellowing could be heard, even back at the camp. Nachezwa's second arrow struck the animal in the back of the neck. This momentarily stunned it and stopped its charge. It again reared up on its hind legs, pawing wildly in the air. This allowed Nachezwa to release a third arrow which struck the bear in the middle of its chest. The bear shuddered, dropped down on all fours and continued coming straight up the slope toward him. The lion remained on the ledge, issuing loud screams, as if waiting for the bear to get in close. Nachezwa knew the ledge would provide him time for possibly two more arrows, before the bear would be upon him. The position of the bear, coming up the hill, wouldn't allow a shot that would kill the beast. An arrow in the big thick hump on his back would not kill or do much damage. Nachezwa knew he must wait until the bear began to pull itself over the ledge at his feet. Even with a plan on how to overcome this gigantic charging beast, he allowed doubt and fear to enter his mind. Up until this moment, anger and adrenaline made him excited enough to challenge the bear. Then he remembered his father's teachings; one must put both fear and anger aside when dealing with the enemy. Fear is not bad if it makes one consider what he is up against. You must then direct the outcome, using judgment derived from fear. Once the situation is in progress, fear only gets in one's way, while anger has no value. Anger drains one's energy and clouds the mind.

With only four arrows remaining, he realized he wouldn't get off more than one, possibly two shots. He also knew it would be either him or the bear. The bear was now directly underneath, just beginning to pull itself upon the ledge. Nachezwa positioned himself to the back of the ledge to allow the arrow to gain some striking power. He kept telling himself to wait until the bear was fully extended, so he could shoot directly at the heart. This, he thought, would be his only way to kill the gigantic animal. Just as the bear made its final effort to pull itself upon the ledge, the lion made its move. Nachezwa released his arrow, hitting the bear in the throat. Just as the arrow struck the bear's throat, the lion sprang forward. All its body weight struck the bear on its upper torso. The combination of the lion's weight and the arrow's impact propelled both the bear and the lion off the ledge. Seeing his adversary disappear backwards off the ledge, Nachezwa ran to its edge. He observed as the two animals tossed and rolled on down the hillside. Dirt flew and undergrowth was thrown in all directions. Both animals were clawing and biting as they continued on down the hill until they struck the rock. All became quiet; it appeared as if the bear was dead. Nachezwa couldn't locate the lion. Satisfied the bear was still, Nachezwa cautiously approached and discovered it to be dead. He saw a slight movement of yellow fur; the lion was pinned against the rock. The weight of the gigantic bear was pressing down upon the lion. Nachezwa attempted to push the bear's dead weight from atop the lion. It proved to be impossible, as he struggled until he was exhausted. He sat upon the rock to regain his strength. A short distance away, he saw the lifeless body of Urr and he suddenly remembered the ring. Once at Urr's side, he slowly lifted his tiny body and gently removed the ring. It felt strange to the touch—soft, yet elastic. It easily stretched off Urr's small neck and up over his much larger head. Nachezwa began to pull the ring down over his own head, then decided to let it remain on the top portion of his head. He had seen many of the warriors with similar looking leather bands. Some were adorned with an eagle feather stuck in their hair. The feather was held in place by the leather band. He had momentarily forgotten the struggle of the pinned lion and basked in the comfortable feeling provided by the ring. Urr's memory was vivid. Urr had left a mental message for Nachezwa which explained that Urr would be dead when Nachezwa came to meet him at the rock. Urr knew it would be a sad experience for Nachezwa to watch him die. Urr had planned for Nachezwa to find his lifeless body at the base of the meeting place rock. The thought then occurred to Nachezwa that the bear did not kill Urr. It must have happened upon Urr's body as it crossed through the meadow. The bear lost its life because of anger. Anger from all, the bear itself, Nachezwa and the lion. It was as Eagle Feather had taught him. Do not let anger direct your actions or you will soon regret the final outcome. The lion attacked the bear for the same reason as Nachezwa. The lion, the lion, oh! Somehow he had momentarily forgotten. The lion was being crushed and suffocated under the weight of the bear. Nachezwa once again was about to struggle moving the bear. He wished for an easier way for the bear to be moved. Nachezwa was taken back when the bear began to float up and away from the rock. It soon settled back on the ground, a few feet away. The lion began to move. It was very wobbly as it arose on its feet. Still dazed, it proceeded over to the head of the bear. Lightly, it pawed at the dead animal's massive head, and made sure the bear was really dead. Once it was satisfied, it took one last glance back at Nachezwa. Its thoughts were basic and primitive. One did not have to wear the ring; its meaning was clear. As if to say we did it, it slowly wandered off.

Nachezwa crawled upon the rock, sitting quietly, allowing his thoughts to be guided by the ring's power. During this period, he was given a brief visual journey of Urr's life. He gained insight into the Smarzon people's plight in their search for the substance URLA. While in this thought process, the memory and teachings of Urr became ingrained within his mind forever. The ring provided subconscious guidance into Nachezwa's brain. It advised him to use these powers only for matters of significant importance. Never, if possible, call attention to yourself, the ring, or its powers.

Knowing he had taken this gigantic animal's life, through an act of mistaken anger, provided him with little or no satisfaction. Nachezwa knew, as with any animal killed by tribe members, nothing would go to waste. Every part of an animal would serve a purpose. He and all the tribe's members were taught this by their fathers and their father's father back to the beginning of time. All life on earth remains precious to the red-skinned man. The tribe's people will benefit from his and the lion's kill. He knew he could transport the large carcass effortlessly with his newly acquired thought power. He himself could fly alongside the carcass back to the campsite. He didn't know why he had chosen to walk back to the campsite and obtain help from the women and his young followers.

When the women and children arrived at the meadow, they saw the gigantic bear lying dead, filled with Nachezwa's arrows. Everyone stood momentarily in awe and disbelief. The eldest of the tribe women, Raven Spirit, broke the silence and spoke praises of this great feat. "The young son of Eagle Feather and Bird Wing, known to us as Nachezwa, has done this great thing without help. He has done what no other single warrior has ever done." She, in all her many summers, had never heard of such a feat, not even at the gathering of the many tribes. "The best of hunters dare not face the mighty bear alone; this bear is the largest I have ever seen. We must protect the hide and head, to show all who come to the gathering place of the many tribes." She continued, "The killing of this mighty bear will give Nachezwa much respect from all the tribe's warriors." After Raven Spirit had finished speaking praises, the women began the task of skinning and preparing the animal's carcass for movement back to camp. They soon had it skinned, with the meat cut into smaller sizes for carrying. It was then loaded on the well worn racks made of bound leather and spruce poles. The youngest of the tribe had already started back to the campsite, laden with burdens almost too heavy for them to carry.

It was near dark when the carriers of the bear meat arrived back at the camp. The tribe's hunting warriors could also be seen coming down off the nearby hillside, returning from their hunt.

Those that remained within the camp were always anxious to greet the returning hunters. This campsite reception had much more excitement ringing in the air, more than any of the previous receptions for past hunts. It was obvious, from the appearance of the returning hunters, their hunt was not as bountiful as they had hoped. The women and children of the tribe were talking at the same time, telling about Nachezwa's giant bear. This commotion required Wolf Paw to command silence. He said, "Let only one voice be heard." He asked Raven Spirit to speak so all could understand. "What has taken place in these past few days to cause this excitement?" Raven Spirit told about Nachezwa's killing of the giant bear. She had several of the women spread the skin out so all could see. The same feeling the women and children had felt, when they first saw the grizzly, also swept over the gathered group of warriors. Two elderly braves did not go on the hunt. They chose to remain at the campsite with the women and children. Even with the gigantic hide spread in front of them, it still seemed impossible that Nachezwa alone had killed such a bear as this. The meat from the bear, and what the hunting party had obtained, pleased Wolf Paw and the other warriors. Dog Fang, though, didn't like all the praise and attention everyone was giving Nachezwa. No one ever gave him the recognition he deserved when he did great things like.... He needed more time to think, but for now he knew it was best to keep his feelings within himself. Especially now, when everyone was excited over Nachezwa's bear. This killing of such a bear by the young Nachezwa didn't help his plans. He still thought he could become chief of all the tribes. This event made anything he had ever done appear insignificant and meaningless. The portion he provided of their hunt's meat was small in comparison. He knew the others hadn't witnessed his several missed attempts at some deer and an elk. That evening the camp rejoiced and several danced around the fire. Wolf Paw gathered all the hunters and held a separate council. They were asked to consider his nephew, son of Eagle Feather, known as Nachezwa, to become a warrior. "We need no further proof of his hunting skills; he should become a warrior." No one disapproved of Wolf Paw's suggestion. Even Dog Fang gave approval for Nachezwa's acceptance as a warrior. They wanted to have Nachezwa tell how he came to kill such an animal. The bear, especially the grizzly, was the most feared and respected of all animals. Nachezwa told the story, leaving out Urr and the mountain lion. His explanation of the entire event was guided mentally by the ring. The ring, during the course of events, had changed its appearance to look like a deerskin head band. Nachezwa's wearing of the head band went unnoticed, as several of the tribe's warriors were also wearing similar-looking head adornments.

Nachezwa received many gifts for his killing of the bear and becoming a warrior. Running Elk offered him his choice of a pony. Badger Face gave him several arrows; Dog Fang even gave a decent beaver pelt. Nachezwa figured Bird Wing could use it to make him a protective winter head cover. The praise, gift giving and merriment went far into the evening. All celebrated this and the coming event of breaking camp. Preparation was underway for their two-day journey and most looked forward to moving to the winter rendezvous area. The winter gathering of the many tribes was usually a good time for everyone in each tribe. This was when the young warriors would often select and barter for their future mate.

It was late into the next day before even the camp dogs were aroused. Wolf Paw had decided they would begin their journey out of the mountains early on the following morning. After the evening merriment, the camp was peaceful and lazy. The tribe's members were pleased with their fruitful summer in the mountains. Wolf Paw spent much of the day wondering where Nachezwa had wandered off. He wanted to talk with him about their moving of the camp. It was while he was trying to locate Nachezwa, he heard of Bird Wing's success in explaining the move. This much pleased Wolf Paw, as he would rather hunt and not have to organize the tribe's activities.

Eagle Feather had always done matters such as this; he wanted Nachezwa to continue in his father's footsteps. Wolf Paw then relaxed, knowing one of the duties he disliked had been taken care of. With the urgency gone, it was later during the day before he located Nachezwa. During his observation of Nachezwa, Wolf Paw could see the young warrior had grown into a man. A man and yes, a warrior, he thought, especially in the short time since the death of his father. Wolf Paw sensed someday Nachezwa would prove to be a chief, possibly even a great chief over all the tribes.

Nachezwa awoke early that next morning; he felt prodded by the ring. Without eating and without even arousing the camp dogs, he quietly slipped out of the camp. Once out of sight, he gently lifted off the ground and flew in the direction the tribe would proceed during their journey to the winter rendezvous. He arrived at the place where they always stopped after their first day of travel. He knew the tribe wouldn't erect their teepees but would camp under some overhanging cliffs. These would provide shelter from any inclement weather. Nachezwa was able to gather and stack a large amount of wood under the protection of the outcropping cliffs. When this was completed, he continued on his flight to the location the leaders selected the previous spring for this winter's rendezvous. None of the other tribes had yet arrived. He knew he could accomplish a lot of work, necessary to insure a good winter encampment. Nachezwa used his powers and moved several distant dead trees into the selected camp site. He knew past winters had proved difficult without sufficient wood for their fires. A large amount of wood was required to provide heat and fuel for cooking. He was able to accomplish in minutes what his tribe's warriors would have taken several days to do. When an ample quantity of wood was gathered, Nachezwa, through his mental powers, moved large chunks of black rock from a nearby quarry. These black rocks were piled into a large stack several feet high. When the stack was complete, a strong beam of light shot forth from Nachezwa's eyes. It struck the pile of rocks with a mighty force. The large rocks were shattered into chunks the size of one's head. Nachezwa wondered why.

Before he received an answer, he flew a short distance from the campsite, opposite the nearby stream. Again, the light from his eyes cut a narrow ditch several feet deep. He then began to mentally transport large quantities of tall dry grasses, placing them near the furrowed-out trench. He also stacked large mounds of this grass in several scattered areas and then transported several more large, dead trees in near the trench. Branches, containing tree growth, were placed to provide a temporary shelter. Once these questionable tasks were accomplished, he returned unobserved a short distance from their camp. As Nachezwa came into view, Running Elk approached him and excitedly requested Nachezwa select the pony he had been promised.

Running Elk allowed Nachezwa the pick of any pony from his herd. It had only been within the last two generations that horses were captured and used for riding and hauling material. Prior to that, they were hunted solely as a source of food. If food became scarce, the horses could be sacrificed to feed the tribes. Running Elk would train and provide for the tribe's horses and, in return, he received hides and foods from all the tribe's families. This would be Nachezwa's own pony, a gift for becoming a warrior. Only warriors were allowed to own a pony. Women and children were forbidden to own one. Nachezwa took his time as he inspected each and every animal. With the mental power provided by the ring, he was able to tell age, health, temperament and strength of each individual pony. Upon completion of his inspection, he selected a small, grey, four-year-old mare. The little mare had all the appearance of being fit and suited for riding and hauling. Nachezwa knew the animal was carrying a colt that would be born sometime in early spring.

Chapter 5

THE JOURNEY TO WINTER CAMP

The morning of the move, everyone was up early, eating, and downing teepees. Excitement filled the air. It was early. The sun hadn't yet shown itself. The process was accomplished without a single hitch. Even the smallest of children were seen assisting in the preparation for this move. Even though things proceeded quickly and smoothly, Wolf Paw appeared worried. He had lived long enough to tell when a major storm was soon to occur. If this happened, it would cause hardship and make the days of travel difficult.

When all the tribe was packed and ready, it had became apparent, to even the smallest child that a major storm was near. None had to be prodded. The procession was on its way, moving in the direction of the lower valley, the winter rendezvous for the many tribes. The morning travel proceeded well. Great gusts of wind slapped at the travelers but failed to slow their progress. The wind gathered moisture and pelted itself hard against these determined people. Temperatures dropped rapidly, to near freezing. The cold penetrated into their bones. Many felt the effects of being chilled. Some wanted to stop, find shelter and wait out the storm. The eldest members encouraged them to continue, they must reach the overhanging cliffs no matter how difficult travel became. Bird Wing sat atop Nachezwa's grey mare; nestled tight in her arms was Pot Dog. Nachezwa walked along side and led a tribe pony that pulled their provisions. Nachezwa and Bird Wing were three families behind the procession leader. The head party consisted of only one person, Dog Fang. Having only himself to worry about, he sat atop his pony, tightly wrapped in furs, dragging his teepee and few provisions. Wolf Paw and Running Elk took up the rear, making sure no one was left behind. Nachezwa sensed it the moment it happened. Dog Fang missed the way to the overhanging cliffs. The trail he chose would lead them to the top of some cliffs. This route, Nachezwa knew, could not be traveled with horses, women, and children, carrying burdensome packs.

Nachezwa immediately stopped the procession. He ran ahead to warn the leading families and Dog Fang. Dog Fang wouldn't listen; he argued he was the more experienced traveler and knew the mountain trails better than Nachezwa. Dog Fang said, "I am going to continue in this direction, the right direction. You and the others can follow me or go your own way, I do not care." Nachezwa ran to the rear and alerted Wolf Paw. He explained what took place at the front of the procession. Wolf Paw and several others moved up to the front of the procession. They could see how one could make the mistake. Some agreed with Dog Fang's directions while most agreed with Nachezwa. Nachezwa convinced Wolf Paw, Running Elk, Badger Face and several of the most respected warriors. He said, "The ledge protection they were seeking was over the next ridge." With visibility so poor they were unable to even see the ridge, it was decided they should go Nachezwa's way; nobody chose to follow Dog Fang. The wind quit and began to drop large, wet snowflakes. They were halfway up on the mountain side, lost in a snow storm, completely enshrouded in the clouds. Nachezwa, and Badger Face led the party as they topped a ridge. It was as Nachezwa had said; in front of them were the cliffs they were searching for. They were soon nestled under the protection of the overhanging cliffs. Badger Face discovered the large stack of dry wood and had quickly built a fire. Heat reflected from off the rock surface and soon several small fires were fed the plentiful dry timber. The wet and weary travelers bedded down for the evening, thankful they'd followed Nachezwa's direction. The storm continued into the night, dropping nearly a foot of snow. By morning, the skies had cleared and the sun began to melt the snow. With the cliff's overhang and the ample supply of wood, they could easily maintain their fires. Once their wet clothing was dried, their joyful spirit returned. They had just begun when Dog Fang could be seen coming over the ridge, looking tired and wet. Wolf Paw motioned for the tribe to proceed; he and two warriors would wait for Dog Fang. The melting snow made their journey slippery, but the terrain wasn't as treacherous as the day before and failed to slow their progress.

Dog Fang told Wolf Paw, "I almost walked over the cliffs in the darkness of the blinding snowstorm. I tried to backtrack to where I was separated from the group, but snow covered your tracks. I had been going in the wrong direction and had to travel all during the night. I just now arrived at this place of these protective cliffs. I am too exhausted to continue." Wolf Paw assigned the two warriors to complete the journey the following day with Dog Fang. Plenty of wood remained to afford them a fire. The two warriors Wolf Paw had selected to stay with Dog Fang did so only because Wolf Paw had directed them to do so.

As the party reached the lower portion of the mountain, the snow disappeared. None had fallen on the lower valley floor. They arrived at the encampment simultaneously with another tribe that had traveled several days coming from the mountain range that lay to the south. It was late afternoon and the weather was pleasant. No one was concerned enough to erect their teepees that evening. Dry timber was plentiful, ample water was in the nearby stream. Large stacks of piled grass were available for their horses. It appeared to be a good winter camp. It was dark when the travel-weary third tribe arrived. They were eager to rest until morning.

The following morning, after their morning meal, most of the travelers allowed time for socializing. Everybody was happy to see one another. The tribes were comprised of several close relations, some as close as brothers, sisters, uncles and cousins. This winter gathering was where most of the braves would usually find a mate. In the spring, the new squaw bride would leave her tribe to join with her husband's tribe. Each spring the tribes would separate from camp and go to the surrounding mountains. They were nomadic and lived off the earth. It wasn't difficult for the new brides, because they knew they would be reunited with their families the next winter. It was a reunion they all looked forward to. In the spring, everyone was ready to return to their summer encampments. The long months of winter were difficult for them. Winters that produced deep snow lasted long into the spring and were hard on everyone. The winters with deep snow on this lower valley floor required an abundance of firewood and food, food enough to feed hundreds of people, numerous camp dogs and many horses. Each winter season the gathering became considerably larger. Three tribes had arrived at the encampment, two more were soon expected. The five tribes were not equal in size; some were nearly twice as large as Wolf Paw's tribe. Three of the tribes were larger and one had less members than Wolf Paw's tribe. Over the years, some tribe members would occasionally separate from the five main tribes. They would go their own way and some were never seen or heard from ever again. Sometimes one or two would return only to search for a mate. Those that left were usually the younger warriors seeking adventure. Others left because they could not comply with the various day-to-day activities required within a large group. For the majority, these gatherings were a time to rejoice.

Chapter 6

CHIEF OF CHIEFS

This was the first winter rendezvous where all the braves from each tribe would gather and decide on a single chief. This chosen chief would reign supreme over all the five tribes. During these winter gatherings his word is law and must be obeyed. Many problems had to be solved now that the gatherings were getting so large. Food, fuel, water, unsanitary conditions, cabin fever, family squabbles, sickness and occasionally arguments amongst the tribe members. The chiefs and other selected individuals formed a council and presented their tribe's problems, offered up solutions and then carried out the chosen chief's decisions. These things were discussed during past winter encampments, but had never been put into place.

It was mid afternoon when the two warriors, whom Wolf Paw had stay with Dog Fang, came riding into camp without Dog Fang. They said, "He acted strange, was crazy in the head, would fight, kick, and yell words they couldn't understand. He would not allow them to bring him into camp." Nachezwa and several other braves heard the report about Dog Fang. Those from other tribes, who knew Dog Fang, had a dislike for him. Some suggested he be left alone to die or wander off. Wolf Paw didn't care for Dog Fang, but he knew Dog Fang didn't deserve to die. Wolf Paw said, "I will ride to the overhanging cliffs and return with Dog Fang."

The ring put thoughts into Nachezwa's mind. Nachezwa reminded Wolf Paw that he was their chief and should remain at the winter camp. He should be here to greet the other two tribes when they arrive. Nachezwa volunteered to go in Wolf Paw's place; he would go alone and return with Dog Fang. He said, "I will first try and talk Dog Fang into returning with me. If talk fails, I will wait until Dog Fang is too ill to resist." Once Wolf Paw was convinced, Nachezwa mounted his pony and rode in the direction of the overhanging cliffs.

Nachezwa rode to the foot of the mountains before he dismounted. Using the ring's power, Nachezwa had his pony graze the surrounding area. Plentiful feed and water were available as snow had yet to fall at this elevation. Nachezwa lifted off the ground and flew towards the cliffs and Dog Fang. To arrive undetected, Nachezwa became invisible before sitting down next to Dog Fang. Dog Fang muttered incoherently, tossing and turning in a delirious fever. Nachezwa knew he could heal Dog Fang using the ring. An opportunity to use Dog Fang's fevered condition could be of benefit. Subconscious thoughts were implanted into Dog Fang's delirious mind. BLACK ROCK BURNS SLOW AND HOT AND ALL WASTE MUST GO INTO THE LONG AND NARROW HOLE.

After Nachezwa spent the evening and most of the next day attending to Dog Fang's fever, he flew Dog Fang, Dog Fang's horse, and Dog Fang's possessions to where his pony grazed. Dog Fang was then tied securely to his teepee. This teepee travois was used to drag Dog Fang to the rendezvous camp. It was early evening when they came riding in. Nachezwa could see the other two tribes had arrived during his absence. Many teepees covered the ground which had stood barren two days earlier. Once in camp, the delirious Dog Fang mumbled: "BLACK ROCK BURNS SLOW AND HOT AND ALL WASTE MUST GO INTO THE LONG AND NARROW HOLE." He repeated this message over and over; it required one to listen closely.

Wolf Paw and several warriors from all the tribes were there to greet Nachezwa and the delirious Dog Fang. Nachezwa was questioned concerning the difficulties he encountered with Dog Fang. Dog Fang continued his muttering. "What is Dog Fang muttering?" one brave asked. Several gathered around Dog Fang to listen. Wolf Paw said, "BLACK ROCK BURNS SLOW AND HOT AND ALL WASTE MUST GO INTO THE LONG AND NARROW HOLE."

All agreed, that was what dog Fang was mumbling! "What does it mean," a young brave asked? Nearly everyone wondered about the large mounds of black rocks and the long narrow hole. Those who selected this gathering site didn't remember the black rocks and the cut in the ground. Nor did they recall the great abundance of dry timber and the abundant piles of dry grass.

Wolf Paw placed a black rock into the fire. A brave whose teepee was near the long narrow hole said, "My squaw has been throwing our spoilage into the hole and kicking loose dirt on top." Nachezwa questioned how Dog Fang knew of these things? He is delirious with fever and has never seen this camp site. This had them all wondering.

With a long branch, Wolf Paw pushed the black rock out of the fire. It glowed red hot and put out much heat. With assistance from Nachezwa, they decided a great spirit was speaking through Dog Fang. All tribe members must use the trench to dispose of unwanted waste. It was Wolf Paw who made the most sense out of Dog Fang's message from the great spirits. It was also Wolf Paw who sent Nachezwa out to get Dog Fang down off the mountain.

Nachezwa, pretending to be tired, entered his teepee that Wolf Paw and Badger Face had put up during his absence. Bird Wing was asleep when Nachezwa became invisible and floated above the main camp fire where several braves were gathered. A powerful light came from Nachezwa's eyes, striking the ground near where they sat. With a voice he himself didn't recognize, he uttered loud and clear,

"Wolf Paw is to become chief of all the gathered tribes. It is I the spirit of all warriors that gave you the black rock that burns, it was I that gave you much dry timber and it was I who made the piles of grass and the narrow hole to place your waste, so as not to spoil the land!" He continued, "All must use the hole in the ground. It will help keep you from the disease and sickness our people have fallen to in the past. I will soon remove the sickness from Dog Fang. You must find a way to cure him of his wicked and evil ways, this I will not do! I will help Wolf Paw make any decision that cannot be decided by your chosen chiefs and thier council."

Not a word was said from any of the braves; a long pause occurred until the silence was interrupted by Dog Fang. Nachezwa had cured Dog Fang, allowing him to wander over to the group assembled around the fire. Dog Fang, no longer delirious, broke the long silence. He asked Wolf Paw, "How did I get out of the blizzard and down off the mountain?"

The only one that questioned whether Wolf Paw should be the chief of all the tribes was Wolf Paw himself.

Nachezwa expected Wolf Paw to be uncomfortable with being the chief. Nachezwa mentally put Wolf Paw at ease because he, the spirit of all warriors, would be there to help guide him.

The next morning, when all the people of the gathering tribes were assembled, it was Wolf Paw they all cheered. No one had failed to hear about the message that came from the Spirit of All Warriors.

Chapter 7

COUNTING COUP

It was during these winter gatherings when the young warriors would usually become uneasy and restless from being restricted by the snow. For some it was difficult to remain in this valley until spring. The winter seemed to pass slowly, as many braves longed for the day they could return to their summer hunting grounds.

Wolf Paw, along with the other chiefs, sensed the restlessness amongst the young, with spring still many moons away. It was mid winter when they developed a game in which all the warriors could engage. A game of mock battles, one tribe's braves stood against another. The smaller tribes would join forces making their battles equal. It became a game of honor, a game of "COUNTING COUP." One could only count coup when he touched the other sides' brave with a weapon. The warrior that had been touched by his enemies' weapon was considered dead. On his honor, he must tell the warrior that killed him his name. He must then remove himself from the battle. The warrior performing the kill could count a coup; one coup for every enemy warrior he touched. The battle would end at the first signs of darkness. A new battle would begin again when the sun was directly overhead. The chiefs could call off the day's battle when they all agreed. Wolf Paw could discontinue the battle anytime. This seldom occurred, as all the braves enjoyed this new sport. Each warrior disliked having their enemy count them as one of the their coup. Once the battle was discontinued because a large herd of buffalo was seen grazing at the far end of the valley. Hunting the buffalo was the most enjoyed hunt of all. The buffalo provided them with meat, clothing, hatchet handles, teepees, moccasins, bedding and blankets for their horses. The tribe's squaws even enjoyed the buffalo hunts. It was during these hunts that the atmosphere was always full with a fervor of excitement. The stories that came from the buffalo hunt were told and listened to from generation to generation. Each hunter had his version of what occurred during the hunt. For days they would celebrate the results of each buffalo hunt; it was always exciting, dangerous, and often entertaining.

The black rock (coal) fuel used to heat and cook was plentiful and made this winter remembered as one of the best. Disposal of all the waste materials, including human waste, made noticeable improvements in the winter campground. When winter was over, the chiefs and the warriors on the council observed that very little sickness had occurred during the winter.

The chiefs of the five tribes decided they would honor the braves who counted the most coup since the sport of the mock battles was established. This they would do before they again disbanded the large gathering and formed into their smaller summer tribes.

It wasn't difficult to decide which warrior had counted the most coup over the winter. Not only did he outnumber even the closest warrior, not once did any warrior ever count coup against him. It was often said by those he counted coup against that Nachezwa was like a ghost. You would never see him until he lightly touched you with his knife, hatchet, or arrow. From out of nowhere Nachezwa would be seen smiling, asking the warrior his name.

The games never went without incident. There were times when actual fighting did occur. However, the fights never did result in more than cuts, bruises and the harboring of harsh feelings toward some individual. This occurred several times before it was finally determined that Dog Fang was always the cause. It appeared that when a warrior would go to "count coup," on Dog Fang, he wouldn't provide his name and remove himself from the game. Also, if Dog Fang was in the position to obtain the "coup," he would strike the warrior with such force it drew blood or inflicted much pain. Before the matter was brought to the attention of Wolf Paw, six braves took it upon themselves to deal with Dog Fang. When Dog Fang ventured out to his chosen spot to begin the day's games, the braves hid themselves from his view. One brave allowed Dog Fang to creep up on him while the others lay hidden. As Dog Fang was about to "count coup," he was attacked and knocked to the ground unconscious. It was hours later when he awoke. His head was clouded with pain, his arms and legs were stretched and secured to stakes driven into the ground. He lay there unable to move for the remainder of that day and far into the next. His yells for help did not go unnoticed. While several braves moved through that area and came upon the staked-out Dog Fang, none offered to remove him from his predicament. Some even stood over him and spat in his face before moving on.

Wolf Paw received word of what happened to Dog Fang that first evening. However, it was not until late the following day before he ventured out to where Dog Fang lay. When he approached Dog Fang, he did not undo his ties but rather sat down beside him in silence for a long period of time. When he finally broke the silence, he spoke softly of the many problems caused by Dog Fang over many seasons that led up to this incident. When Dog Fang tried to explain his side, he was told to remain silent, to listen and listen good. He would have no say in this matter and would have no say in the future, not until he had proven himself worthy. "Your existence lies totally within my power. No more harm shall befall you if you live without evil in your deeds. If I hear of even a single evil deed in which you are engaged, I will leave your fate up to any and every warrior that winters with us at this gathering. It is your choice, this I promise!" With this said, he cut Dog Fang's ties and walked back to his teepee.

The braves often discussed the day's battle; how many coups they could count on; what if they were eliminated; could they win, etc. They spoke often of how they were amazed when Nachezwa would appear from behind even the most sparse of cover and proclaim them dead. Some said, "He was as swift as an eagle." He would silently tap you from behind, much like the mighty eagle would strike its prey. When he would proclaim a coup, the dead brave would often yell out loud, warning others nearby he had just been killed as if by a swift and silent white eagle.

This was Nachezwa's first winter as a warrior. The braves from the other tribes knew another name would be selected for Nachezwa by his tribe's chief. It seemed as if Nachezwa was as swift and deadly as the mighty eagle, the one with the white head. All agreed he should become known by the name, "White Eagle." The band around Nachezwa's head took on a lighter color, grey white in appearance, and he found two large, white eagle feathers to adorn his head band.

Chapter 8

SPOTTED FAWN

It was near the end of the winter when Bird Wing noticed a young Indian squaw from the large Northern tribe. Bird Wing could see her distinct moccasins, like many from that tribe, whose chief was called Standing Buffalo. It was this winter they came to be known as Black Feet of Standing Buffalo's tribe. Most of the tribe members wore the knee length moccasins, made from the heavy thick hide of the dark buffalo. This gave the appearance that their feet and lower legs were black. The young squaw would often appear in the area surrounding Wolf Paw's tribe. Bird Wing wondered whether Nachezwa had taken notice of the comely one they called Spotted Fawn. Nachezwa was seldom around the teepee during the day. He was always playing the warrior game of counting coup or he was gone for several days, hunting buffalo. One morning, Spotted Fawn, with two of her friends, wanted to see the great warrior brave, the one her brother called White Eagle. Spotted Fawn told Bird Wing that White Eagle had killed her brother many times and counted the most coup in the mock battles. Bird Wing hadn't paid much attention to this new winter activity. She told Spotted Fawn her warrior son was called Nachezwa, until their tribe chief gave him a final name. she knew of no warrior in their tribe named White Eagle. Spotted Fawn said that all the braves in the Black Feet of Standing

Buffalo's tribe often spoke of this warrior, the one who alone killed the mighty grizzly bear. The mighty White Eagle had even done this before his tribe had proclaimed him a warrior. Bird Wing then knew Spotted Fawn was referring to her son Nachezwa.

Bird Wing called for Nachezwa to come out from the teepee and see his visiting admirers. With sleep-filled eyes, Nachezwa threw back the heavy buffalo skin. It kept the opening covered and kept out the cold winter winds. There stood three young beautiful Indian maidens from the tribe of Black Feet of Standing Buffalo's tribe. This immediately brought him awake and filled with embarrassment. Having taken the ring off during sleep, here he was faced with three members of the opposite sex, dumbfounded, without support from the ring. Bird Wing noticed that Nachezwa was unable to speak. When Nachezwa finally spoke, he uttered more sounds than words. It brought a big smile on Bird Wing's face as she watched her young sons fumble in words and actions. She thought to herself, "The mighty White Eagle, counter of much coup, struck dumb by three young, meek and beautiful maidens." It became evident to Bird Wing that Spotted Fawn caused his feeling of confusion. Nachezwa wanted and missed his headband. Being unable to think, he remained embarrassed. Somehow he managed to get through this event, though tongue tied, weak in the knees and feverish. He had thoughts of Dog Fang flashing through his mind; he knew he was mumbling badly and he didn't even speak a message. He had nothing of importance to say, but the maidens didn't seem to notice Nachezwa was uncomfortable around them. Bird Wing could see they were also in another world of their own. It seemed as if all they could do was giggle. They would frequently place their hand to their mouths as if they too were embarrassed. In spite of it all, it was refreshing to watch these young people. It took a comment from Running Elk to bring the situation back to normal. Running Elk told Nachezwa that his grey mare had given birth to a new colt during the night. Running Elk said, "I am about to go see if everything is all right with your mare and its newborn, do you want to come see them?"

Nachezwa excused himself from the three maidens and caught up with Running Elk. He wanted to visit his pony and her new colt. This birth of a new colt proved exciting enough to disrupt Nachezwa and Spotted Fawn's first encounter. Somehow, Nachezwa and Spotted Fawn knew this would not be their last meeting.

Both Bird Wing and Running Elk, for some unexplained reason, spent the rest of the day unaware they were smiling. Try as he may, Nachezwa, for some reason, never felt worse. The power of the ring didn't even seem to help.

As Running Elk and Nachezwa approached the area where the horses were grazing, Nachezwa's grey pony came as if being called. She trotted over to Nachezwa. Trailing behind her came the newborn on very wobbly legs. Seeing the weak, beautiful little animal made the feverish effect Spotted Fawn had on him disappear.

Wolf Paw, Standing Buffalo and the other tribe's chiefs were preparing to ride southwest in search of next season's rendezvous site. Wolf Paw invited Nachezwa to ride along with him and the other chiefs. Without hesitation, Nachezwa mounted one of the tribe's many horses. Nachezwa felt honored, he being the only warrior chosen by the Chief of All the Tribes to accompany him and the other chiefs. It was an honor to help select the site of their next year's camp.

They rode for most of the day, stopping to view

several areas suitable for the next winter's encampment. Wolf Paw and the other four chiefs appeared puzzled and unable to select one from the sites they had visited. Nachezwa, sensing their disappointment, questioned why they were unable to select a future place to gather the five tribes.

Wolf Paw, the Chief of Chiefs, exclaimed that none had the available firewood, black rock that burns, and the long narrow ditch for placing their waste. Nachezwa appeared to be thinking, but soon said that each of the chiefs should pick the camp they preferred. When they returned back to the main camp, each should pray to the "Spirit Of All Warriors," and ask for his guidance in providing these things. This answer seemed to satisfy all the chiefs. Nachezwa knew that one campsite they had visited was superior to the others. They returned in darkness and each chief went to their separate teepee to pray to the Spirit Of All Warriors.

Allowing each chief adequate time to pray, Nachezwa became invisible and again flew above the central fire. With a display similar to the Northern Lights, he called for the chiefs to assemble. Using the deep Erie voice, once they were all present, Nachezwa spoke to them and convinced them to select the best campsite for the following winter. Each chief thought that the "Spirit Of All Warriors" had answered his prayer. All had made the same selection. The "Spirit Of All Warriors" also stated that wood, black rock, the deep narrow trench, along with a surprise would be provided for their next winter's gathering. "NEXT WINTER, WILL BE THE LAST TIME I WILL PROVIDE FOR YOU. I HAVE SHOWN AND TAUGHT YOU WHAT CAN AND MUST BE DONE. YOU MUST NOW LEARN AND DO FOR YOURSELVES." Once his message was completed, the

Northern Light display disappeared and all became silent. The chiefs and several braves gazed into the night sky that held the twinkle of the distant stars.

Before sun up, Nachezwa was on his way flying to the selected campsite. He gathered the big dead trees and obtained a large pile of the black rock that burns. In moments, the long, deep and narrow trench was carved in the ground. He gathered the long, dead grasses and with wet clay he soon assembled a hut made of these materials, aided with a few branches of a tree. He then scooped out a circular section of earth a few feet deep and lined it with river rocks. Aided by a laser blast, a hidden underground hot spring of pungent smelling water began to flow and make its way into this circular basin. He cut squares of sod, using the beam of light from his eyes. With the sod, he soon had assembled another hut that resembled the first, this one built directly over the circular basin which was nearly full of the steamy sulfur and mineral water. Once the basin was full, he cut another portion out of the earth which allowed the overflow to return to its natural underground channel. With these things completed, he returned to camp. This was all accomplished even before the camp dogs had begun to arouse. The smallest of camp dogs, the one Nachezwa called Pot Dog, had been sleeping just inside the fold of their teepee's large, heavy Buffalo skin. Since Pot Dog was kind of an outcast from the other camp dogs, he had became attached to Bird Wing and Nachezwa. During the cold winter evenings, Pot Dog became their teepee's flap weight. This amused Bird Wing and Nachezwa; it did help keep the stronger winter winds from blowing open the buffalo flap and gusting into their teepee. Pot Dog took the liberty to act in this capacity. He soon become accustomed to choice bits of scraps from both Nachezwa and Bird Wing.

It was early morning when Spotted Fawn stood nearby watching Bird Wing prepare the morning meal. Bird Wing noticed the presence of the young maiden. She so enjoyed witnessing the previous day's activities and awkwardness of her son around the three young maidens. Bird Wing immediately invited Spotted Fawn to join her and Nachezwa for their morning meal. Nachezwa, just arousing from sleep, was unaware of his early morning visitor.

Nachezwa gave a big tug on the heavy flap of their teepee before he could step outside. He gave forth with a yawn, his eyes still full of sleep. He was very mindful not to step on this winter's flap weight, Pot Dog. He thought to himself, "How did this scruffy little animal work its way into he and Bird Wing's hearts?" This was unheard of, this brown ball of fur had become considered almost family. With the loss of his father, Pot Dog had helped fill some of that emptiness for both him and his mother. Nachezwa was completely outside the teepee when he remembered he was without his special head band. He then noticed a startling, yet pleasant surprise. There beside Bird Wing, stood the young maiden Spotted Fawn. Ever since their first encounter, she seemed to have an overwhelming affect on him. He easily became flushed in the face, awkward of speech and physically weak in the knees. Spotted Fawn also appeared somewhat the same. She displayed her nervousness with flushed cheeks, a large grin, and try as she might, she could not contain the frequent giggles.

Bird Wing observed the young Indian maiden and her son. She was very proud of him, the newest brave and warrior recently given the name "White Eagle." Nachezwa wanted so badly to return to the teepee and obtain his ring head band, but could not do so without drawing attention.

Bird Wing finally interrupted the long awkward silence by placing food within their reach. The silence was finally broken with sounds of their eating. If one listened hard, some semblance of conversation slowly began to develop. By the time all had eaten the morning meal, the young couple slowly began feeling comfortable with one another.

Bird Wing, sensing she was no longer needed, went on about her business. Both youngsters failed to miss her absence. Their full attentions were directed toward each other. Before the day was done, both knew much about the other and several tribe members' varied strengths and weaknesses. They even wasted some of their precious time discussing Dog Fang. Seen through the eyes of those they encountered, these two youngsters were obviously developing a strong fondness for each other.

During this day of their getting acquainted, they noticed a scouting party ride into camp. The party's leader was anxious to report their findings to the Chief of Chiefs, Wolf Paw. "Good News! We spotted a herd of Buffalo, just a short day's journey away. The herd is grazing peacefully and unlikely to move on. The grazing grasses are abundant and should support this size herd for several days." The chiefs gathered the scouting warriors and discussed how to prepare for this hunt. It was decided that early the next morning all the encampment's warriors would engage in the hunt. Only the elderly, the women, and the young would remain behind. This would be the season's final combined tribe's buffalo hunt. Soon they would separate into the smaller tribes and return to their summer hunting grounds.

White Eagle, as with all the chiefs and warriors, enjoyed the buffalo hunt; even the women and children seemed to relish these hunts. It provided sport and excitement, and it always included danger. Often the hunters would get hurt or even killed when the gigantic beasts began to stampede. To the Indian, the buffalo proved to be the most valuable of animals. The buffalo provided most of the needs for all the tribes' many people. From the hides, they were able to make many articles of clothing, footwear, teepee bottoms and flaps. The horns were used in food preparation and for knife handles. The beasts' tail hair was often braided into a rope. The animal's bladders were used to store water, the skulls were used as adornments around the encampment. The medicine man seemed to make the most use of this animal's remains. But most precious to all was the meat; it staved off hunger and provided the most wonderful of tastes. Buffalo meat was not so strong to one's taste as the elk, deer and bear.

That next morning the tribe's members were assembled to watch the largest ever of hunting parties depart. The entire hunt was to be accomplished under the leadership of Wolf Paw! Wolf Paw knew silence, stealth and surprise were their best weapons. Spotted Fawn stood beside Bird Wing and waved goodbye to White Eagle and to her father Black Crow and her brother, Grey Hawk. Both the young warriors, White Eagle and Grey Hawk, were riding side by side. They had become friends over the winter during the games of counting coup. Grey Hawk was proud of his sister for gaining such favored attention of the games most successful player, Nachezwa, the White Eagle.

Chapter 9

THE BUFFALO HUNT

They rode until the sun had passed the middle of the sky, toward the destination where the scouts had previously seen the herd of buffalo. It was mid afternoon when they stopped to camp. They remained at a considerable distance from the herd's last location. This distance was necessary so as not to alarm any of the herd's matriarchs or old bulls. Often these mature animals would graze on the outside perimeter of the herd. The hunting party planned to attack the herd at mid morning, which allowed the scouts time to go forward and observe the best method of attack. It also provided the hunters a chance to rest and sleep. It was almost eerie, as many hunters as ever assembled. Yet, White Eagle could hear the sound of birds and many small animals amongst their party's silence.

Wolf Paw said, "The four scouts and White Eagle are to go toward the herd at varied points. Each will observe the herd without being discovered, and gather information to aid our hunt." These scouts rode quietly away as Wolf Paw had directed. White Eagle rode in the direction determined to be toward the head of the herd. Once he was out of sight, he slid down off his pony. He became invisible and flew the short distance to the large body of animals grazing in the deep grasses. As he soared above the herd, he observed that far off, toward the direction of the setting sun, lay a large swell in the ground. Passing over this area, he observed a place where the ground rapidly fell away. It contained a drop off over two ponies high. Rocks and rough terrain lay hidden at the bottom. This sharp drop would be totally hidden from the view of any buffalo engaged in a stampede.

White Eagle flew over the length of the entire herd, to observe the other scouts. Each scout could be seen watching the herd from some vantage point. The scout, Red Pony, had ridden off toward the tail of the herd. White Eagle could see Red Pony as he lay hidden in the tall grass. Red Pony had positioned himself a great distance from his horse, well hidden from view of the herd. A large bull, grazing a considerable distance from the herd, discovered Red Pony lying there in the tall grass. The bull wasted little time in making a direct assault upon the helpless scout. The bull cut off Red Pony's route of escape. Before White Eagle could destroy this lone bull, it caught Red Pony from the rear, and threw him high into the air. White Eagle managed to catch the unconscious scout and carried him to safety. The bull stood there confused. It had a questioning look in its eyes; where had he thrown the man thing? He soon continued on toward the main herd, moving slowly, appearing as if nothing had happened.

Once the danger passed, White Eagle revived the unconscious scout. He observed Red Pony holding and shaking his head as he slowly limped toward the spot he'd left his horse. Seeing Red Pony was able to make his way back, he then returned to his own grey mare. White Eagle was the last scout to return. Red Pony was first, having already related his story. Red Pony's last memory of the event was: "While I was running toward my horse, I was struck hard from the rear by this huge old bull. I remember being tossed high into the air. I must have struck my head because that is all I can remember. When I came to, the bull was gone. I found myself lying a good distance from where the bull caught up to me." This made sense to those who heard Red Pony's story. It was obvious he had been struck extremely hard. His entire body ached with every step he took. White Eagle would heal Red Pony when all were asleep so Red Pony could join in tomorrow's hunt.

Each of the scouts had explained what they had observed; White Eagle waited until last. He said, "I rode far out in front of the herd where I discovered a drop in the ground. I think that during the hunt the largest body of warriors should attack near the front of the herd. This will force the herd to run toward the direction which the sun goes before darkness. Several stampeding beasts should not survive a fall where the ground rapidly falls away." Wolf Paw, the chief, and the other scouts accepted this as a good plan.

All seasoned hunters knew it was difficult to drop one of these animals, especially while riding at full gallop. Each chief explained the plan to their braves and it was accepted without question. The following morning, each of the tribes' members took their positions. By mid morning, upon the signal from Wolf Paw, the charge on the buffalo had begun. It was only a brief moment in time, the hunt went fast and furious. Buffalo could be seen running in all directions. The main body did turn and run toward the direction where the sun would set. Wolf Paw, from his vantage point, could see animals being felled when struck by many arrows. The hunt was accomplished with success and no one appeared to be hurt. Many of the buffalo had done just as White Eagle had predicted. Some of the hunters managed to bring down a buffalo, but it most often required several arrows to drop a single animal. However, many buffalo never survived the fall where the ground had broken away. Based on the memories of the tribe's member, this was the most successful hunt ever! Little or nothing would go to waste. The animals were quickly skinned and cut up in preparation for moving. The travois's were soon attached to several horses to facilitate the haul back to the main camp.

Days of feasting and rejoicing followed. With this great bounty happening near the end of winter, it prolonged their stay in this lower valley for several more days. This allowed each warrior the chance to tell his version of what occurred during this brief, but most successful of hunts. Everyone's story usually included the plan of attack developed by White Eagle. Even Dog Fang had changed and rejoiced at the success of the hunt. He had seen what could be achieved with everyone working together. During the hunt, he tried in vain to bring down a large bull by himself. It was only accomplished when two of the braves that had staked him to the ground decided to help him defeat one of the mighty animals.

Wolf Paw and all the tribes' chiefs bestowed much praise upon White Eagle. White Eagle managed not to allow all this praise and glory to go to his head. He somehow made all feel as if they too would have made this same decision if they had been given scouting duties directed toward the front of the herd.

Chapter 10

RETURN TO THE MOUNTAINS

Soon, the tribes would again separate and return to their summer hunting grounds. Most agreed that the tribe's people had grown greatly in size during their life time. The wise ones knew that someday this valley would not support all the people of the five tribes. Each summer, the tribes would travel further and further to find new places with game enough to feed their people. Someday, it would be too far for whole tribes of people to travel for a winter gathering.

White Eagle and Spotted Fawn both hated to see this season end. But White Eagle enjoyed the mountains and looked forward to the coming summer and hunting with his fellow warriors. However, he disliked the thought of being separated any long distance from Spotted Fawn. He vowed to Spotted Fawn that during the next winter's gathering, he would make her his squaw and would provide her with the finest of teepees. He also promised he would ride his grey pony, however many day's journey, to visit her and her family. This pleased Black Crow and his family, as they had come to very much like White Eagle and his mother Bird Wing.

During the evenings of this winter encampment, White Eagle, while invisible, used the ring's great healing powers. He made sure to benefit those people most in need. He managed to visit every teepee of every tribe and heal any sickness and correct deformities. Also, while utilizing this power, he gained insight into the tribe's people, their individual strengths and weaknesses. It was during these visits that he learned about the true cause of his father's death. Wolf Paw often discussed with his squaw how he and Eagle Feather had told Dog Fang not to shoot the bear. Dog Fang, however, disregarded their orders and shot the bear. Dog Fang thought if he killed the bear by himself, it would bring him great honor. His wounding the bear proved him to be a coward. Dog Fang could not be forced by either Wolf Paw or Eagle Feather to pursue and finish off the wounded animal. Dog Fang said, "I would rather see the animal suffer than take a chance on the bear killing me." Wolf Paw and Eagle Feather had determined Dog Fang could not be made to complete the task. Both agreed the bear should no longer be required to suffer. It was then decided, by the act of throwing stones, that Eagle Feather would be the one to put the beast out of its suffering and misery. While throwing the stones, the bear could be heard emitting painful bellows. The stones chose Eagle Feather. Wolf Paw wouldn't accept the stones' decision. It would instead be decided by throwing their knives at a nearby tree. The closest to a swirl in the trunk would be the one to pursue the bear.

Wolf Paw most often won these contests over Eagle Feather. This time it was Eagle Feather's knife that flew true to the target. Eagle Feather now had to decide whether he or Wolf Paw would complete the task of killing the beast. Eagle Feather chose himself. "I alone will complete the task and put the wounded beast out of its misery. When I accomplish this task, we will then decide the fate of Dog Fang." The bear had changed the outcome of Dog Fang's fate with the death of Eagle Feather. Wolf

Paw, for reasons not even known to himself, chose not to expose Dog Fang's cowardice to the tribe members. However, he would always keep a watchful eye in matters of importance when they included Dog Fang.

Wolf Paw always wished he had not honored that knife contest. He wished he had gone and finished the bear himself. He knew he was the better hunter. He said, "Eagle Feather was always the thinker, the planner and would have risen to the position of chief of all the five tribes." Nothing would have pleased Wolf Paw more than to see Eagle Feather become Chief of all Chiefs. They should have thrown Dog Fang's fate to the bear. Dog Fang had proven himself to be of no value.

White Eagle, overhearing Wolf Paw, now knew the true story of the death of his father. He knew someday he would deal with the cowardice of Dog Fang. He developed within his mind various ways of dealing with Dog Fang. He would burn his feet with the laser beam and scorch his eyes until he was blind. The band around his head began to constrict so tight he writhed in pain. The pain was so swift and sever he immediately knew the ring would not allow him to do this. It was as Urr had said, "The ring will not perform deeds of evil." This was a small reminder to White Eagle. White Eagle knew Wolf Paw had dealt with Dog Fang while he was staked to the ground. If Dog Fang failed with the advice given him by Wolf Paw, his plight will be decided by members of the many tribes. He then decided if Dog Fang performed evil deeds during the summer camp, he would then deal with the problem, and it would be without help from the ring of Urr.

Even after the ring inflicted a severe, but temporary, pain on him, he still remained infuriated. Since Dog Fang's ignorance and cowardice were the cause of his father's death, he would use the ring to read Dog Fang's mind. Urr had advised him to restrain himself when using this power. With this advice, he had decided not to intrude into others' private thoughts. However, he would make an exception with regards to Dog Fang. He would wait until he could control his anger and contempt for Dog Fang. The only way he could control his anger was by turning his thoughts to Spotted Fawn. Many times he had been tempted to read Spotted Fawn's mind, but decided to leave this alone. He thought the ring and Urr had something to do with his decision.

Deep in thought, White Eagle was startled when Bird Wing shook him. She said, "Wolf Paw has decided our tribe will prepare for the return to the mountains the next morning."

White Eagle spent most of his time that day with Spotted Fawn and her father Black Crow. White Eagle explained to Black Crow his intentions regarding Spotted Fawn. He also requested information as to where their tribe was planning to make summer camp. Black Crow not being their tribe's chief, could only give him a general idea. Their chief, Standing Buffalo, had not decided. Black Crow provided White Eagle with the location of his favored site and said, "If you decide to visit and cannot locate our camp, use signals of smoke. Someone will surely see your signal. Then I, or Grey Hawk will soon answer." White Eagle did not worry, as he knew he could fly and explore great distances within a short time.

It made White Eagle lonely and sad when he said his last goodbye to Spotted Fawn. White Eagle and Bird Wing prolonged their time to leave by volunteering to take up the rear of the tribe's procession. As the tribe moved down the trail, White Eagle felt a tinge of sorrow. He wondered if he would ever see Spotted Fawn again. He already missed her bright smile and infectious laughter and they were only approaching the base of the mountains. If he felt this forlorn with their being less than a day apart, he wondered how he would ever survive the summer. Once they arrived and selected their camp, his mood improved. White Eagle busied himself setting up teepees and assisting others in getting established. He made little use of the ring and eventually his mind wandered to thoughts of Spotted Fawn.

Chapter 11

THE JOURNEY TO SPOTTED FAWN

It was mid summer when White Eagle's restlessness, in wanting to see Spotted Fawn, became so strong he could no longer wait. He discussed his plans with Bird Wing and Wolf Paw. Both of them knew he would no longer wait. They saw him off, cautioned him to take care, as he would be traveling alone.

His heart pounded heavily when he left the grey mare to graze on the grasses of the valley floor. He flew high above the mountains invisible to any eyes. The sun was directly overhead when he located Standing Buffalo's camp. Excited, he returned to his pony and proceeded to send out signals of smoke. Before they could return signals, he rode forward to shorten the distance in the direction of their camp. Keeping his eyes on the skyline, he observed white putts of smoke.

Along his path of travel, he came upon a small mountain lake. Its cool, blue shimmering water, made him aware of the sun's hot rays pouring down upon him. This lake provided an opportunity to bathe and remove the soil from his clothing. A short stop would give his mare needed water and rest. He had traveled a considerable distance since making the signals of smoke. Knowing a hasty arrival would require explaining, a short rest and a wash would be good. This would allow his arrival one of being clean and refreshed.

He removed his clothing, soaked and scrubbed them on some smooth rocks as he had often seen Bird Wing do. He placed them to dry amongst the branches of a scrub oak tree. He removed his head band and placed it on a rock near the water's edge. He welcomed the coolness as he dove into the placid water.

As he swam, he took notice of several large eagles. Each bore the distinction of having the magnificent white head. He enjoyed watching them lazily soar overhead in search of an unwary fish. One swiftly dove toward the surface of the water and easily grasped a trout in its talons. The big bird, with its prey held tight in its grip, easily flew over the tall pines and out of sight. Having experienced flight, he knew the great power and boundless feeling of freedom it provided. He was glad he was given his name, White Eagle, named after this large and powerful bird. He was also glad he was chosen by the people from the heavens to receive and wear the magical ring. He had gotten to know Urr and learn about his people's plight. He had experienced much joy in his few short years of life, more so since receiving the ring. He watched as another of the magnificent birds dove close to the lake's shore. It returned to the skies; held tightly in its powerful claws was a squirrel who had been curiously sniffing at his precious head band. He continued to watch the hapless animal struggle in a futile effort to free itself from the bird's deadly talons. He was again amused when another eagle made a swift downward dive toward his stretched and drying articles of clothing. It was then he experienced overwhelming emotion, the feelings of both pain and fear. What he felt hurt even more than the pain he suffered when he had evil thoughts concerning Dog Fang. The fear was even greater than the fear he experienced when he awaited the arrival of the charging bear.

He felt totally drained, and stared in disbelief. The eagle was now on its upward ascent. Clutched tightly in its powerful grip...THE RING OF URR.

He got out of the water and perched himself on a rock at the lake's edge. With eyes that were glazed over, he stared down into the shimmering water. He had watched the great bird disappear from his sight. Like the others, it flew in the direction from where the sun begins its journey across the vast expanse of heaven and sky off toward those lofty peaks, some so high they still showed signs of last winter's snow. He sat there for the longest time as if in a trance. His clothes had long been dry when he finally began to move. Thinking back, he recalled things he had accomplished, many without the help of the ring. He realized he still had instilled within his mind the memory of Urr.

Urr would always be with him, helping him make the right decisions. Even though he was still in shock from loss of the ring, he was aware of the strength and understanding the ring and Urr had provided. He knew a search for the ring was near hopeless, but he knew he would search!

His thoughts shifted from the ring and toward Spotted Fawn and her family. He knew they awaited him with great joy of love and friendship. Having gained many friends amongst the warriors of their tribes helped ease the painful feelings from losing the ring. He knew he was blessed with good health and the wisdom acquired during the short period he was privileged to wear the ring.

White Eagle put on his clothes and rode toward Spotted Fawn and his many awaiting friends.

THE END

EPILOGUE

White Eagle, at the following winter rendezvous, made Spotted Fawn his squaw. She bore him two proud sons and a daughter. Over the course of time, White Eagle became Chief of Chiefs and proved himself to be a wise and revered leader. For several years he searched in vain for the Ring of Urr. His searching diminished over time, until in his later life he discontinued the search completely. He never revealed to anyone that the ring ever existed. Because of his loss of the ring's power, he'd discovered that he, himself, possessed great strength, wisdom, and courage.

Nearly a hundred years have passed since White Eagle lived and hunted the ravines and meadows hidden beneath lofty mountain peaks. The era of the red-skinned warriors has given way to another breed of man. Men whose eyes do not hold the beauty of the land and its creatures sacred. They looked at these things only as an endless source of power and wealth. The furs and pelts taken from the animals they killed were used only as a source of trade for money and commodities. They hunted the beaver and fox until they became nearly extinct. Most animals were hunted only for their hides. An animal's meat was very seldom used for food and was discarded to rot in the sun.

The weight of his pack wore heavy on the young trapper's shoulders. It could not hold the weight of another fur. He could barely carry it on his back. He made his way down along the stream. He planned to rest where the stream entered the small lake. It was still a consider-able distance and he was extremely tired. Suddenly, he noticed a small, strange object that lay just under the water's surface. He would have to remove the burden-some pack before he could retrieve and examine it. A large boulder stood nearby. He could remove his pack and rest it on the boulder. Should he stop and remove the heavy pack or should he move on? He stood staring down at the object trying to decide.